STORIES OF
FORGIVENESS

Published in the United States of America by Cherry Lake Publishing
Ann Arbor, Michigan
www.cherrylakepublishing.com

Content Adviser: Satta Sarmah Hightower, www.sattasarmah.com
Reading Adviser: Marla Conn MS, Ed., Literacy specialist, Read-Ability, Inc.

Photo Credits: ©Kikovic/Thinkstock Images, cover, 1; ©Iakov Filimonov/Shutterstock Images, 5; ©nrey/Shutterstock
Images, 7; ©Wikimedia, 8; ©Wikimedia, 11; ©Wikimedia, 12; ©Buckvoed/Wikimedia, 15; ©mppriv/Thinkstock Images, 16;
©Nick Ut, 17; ©Edicions La Veu del País Valencià, 18; ©Aussie~mobs/Flickr, 21; ©Fon Hodes/Shutterstock Images, 22;
©Antonella865/Dreamstime Images, 25; ©Trocaire/Flickr, 26; ©Trocaire/Flickr, 28

Library of Congress Cataloging-in-Publication Data has been filed and is available at catalog.loc.gov

Cherry Lake Publishing would like to acknowledge the work of The Partnership for 21st Century Learning.
Please visit *www.p21.org* for more information.

Printed in the United States of America
Corporate Graphics

ABOUT THE AUTHOR

Jennifer Colby is a school librarian in Michigan. She works hard to forgive
others and to ask others to forgive her.

TABLE OF CONTENTS

CHAPTER 1
What Is Forgiveness?........................... 4

CHAPTER 2
Corrie ten Boom 6

CHAPTER 3
Nobuo Fujita and the
Town of Brookings, Oregon 10

CHAPTER 4
Kim Phúc 14

CHAPTER 5
Ray Minniecon and
the "Stolen Children"......................... 20

CHAPTER 6
Hutus and Tutsis 24

THINK ABOUT IT.. 30
FOR MORE INFORMATION.. 31
GLOSSARY 32
INDEX 32

What Is Forgiveness?

Have you ever been ashamed of something you have done? Has anyone ever been mean to you? In both cases, a little bit of forgiveness would help. You can forgive people when you stop blaming them for something they did wrong. You can be forgiven when someone accepts your apology. Many people have forgiven and been forgiven for horrible acts. It takes a lot of love and acceptance to forgive someone who has hurt you. But forgiveness allows you to move on and be happy in life.

Sometimes we need to see things from someone else's point of view.

Corrie ten Boom

Peoples' noble actions can be seen as criminal, depending on the authority in charge. During World War II, the Nazis were capturing **Jewish** Dutch citizens. The ten Booms, a Dutch family, saw it as their duty to harbor these citizens. The family helped many of them escape the **Holocaust**. But the ten Booms were eventually caught and arrested by the Nazis. Years later, a daughter of the family, Corrie, forgave two of her **captors** and their actions. Her story encourages others to be forgiving as well.

Corrie ten Boom was born in 1892 to a family of watchmakers in Haarlem, North Holland, in the Netherlands. In May 1942, they began hiding Jews in a secret room of their house. At any given time, there were five or six people hiding there. This meant that there were a lot of extra mouths to feed at a time of strict

At the start of the war, the Netherlands didn't want to fight but was invaded by Germany anyway.

food **rationing**. Ration cards were available only to non-Jewish Dutch citizens.

One day, Corrie went to the ration card office and mistakenly asked the man in charge for 100 cards instead of the five cards her family was allowed to receive. The man was the father of a disabled girl she had helped in the past. She was given the extra cards without question, and she proceeded to hand out a card to every Jewish person she met.

In February 1944, a Dutch citizen told the Nazis of the ten Booms' secret work, the Nazis found their extra ration cards,

Corrie ten Boom was the first licensed female watchmaker in the Netherlands.

and the entire family was arrested and imprisoned. While in prison, Corrie received a letter simply saying, "All the watches in your cabinet are safe." The six Jews hiding in their house at the time of the arrest had not been discovered, and they later escaped to safety. After a quick trial, Corrie and her sister Betsie were sent to a **concentration camp** in Germany. Their father had already died while in prison.

Corrie and her sister were prisoners in the camp for many months, and in December 1944, Betsie died. Only 15 days later, Corrie was released from the camp. She later learned that she was only freed because an office worker had made an error. All the other women in her age group had died at the camp.

Ten Boom returned home after the war, and she continued to help others by setting up houses for displaced Jews who had survived the war. Ten Boom also assisted jobless Dutch citizens who previously worked for the Nazis. But the most surprising thing she did was to travel to Germany to forgive two male employees of the concentration camp who had been cruel to her and her sister. She saw one of them at a church service in Munich. He bowed to her and offered to shake her hand. Though unwilling at first, she felt love and embraced forgiveness when she returned the gesture.

For 30 years, ten Boom traveled to more than 60 countries to tell her story and encourage forgiveness. She said: "Forgiveness is the key that unlocks the door of resentment and the handcuffs of hatred. It is a power that breaks the chains of bitterness and the shackles of selfishness." Corrie ten Boom died on her birthday in 1983 at the age of 91. Her actions truly symbolize the spirit of forgiveness.

Nobuo Fujita and the Town of Brookings, Oregon

War is horrible. Soldiers in battle sometimes commit unforgivable acts. Yet the only pilot to ever bomb American shores was later forgiven by the small Oregon community he attacked. Born in 1911, Nobuo Fujita was a Japanese pilot who in 1942 flew bombing runs over Brookings, Oregon. In later years, ashamed of his actions, Fujita traveled to Brookings to ask for the town's forgiveness.

During World War II, Japanese military commanders hatched a plan. They would force the American military to focus on protecting its own shores. This would divert its attention and resources away from the conflict in Japan. Fujita suggested the raids, and twice he bombed the forested land surrounding

Fujita poses with his airplane 'Glen.'

Brookings. He was the only Japanese pilot to do this. He left from a Japanese submarine hidden in the Pacific Ocean off the coast of Oregon and dropped multiple bombs. The goal was to start a massive forest fire. Neither bombing mission caused much damage, and no one died, but Fujita was later full of regret for what he had done.

In 1962, Fujita presented the town with his family's 400-year-old **samurai** sword. It had been passed down through the generations, and he had carried it with him throughout the war. He was surprised that the town easily forgave him.

One Brookings mayor proclaimed May 25 'Nobuo Fujita Day.'

The mayor once said of Fujita, "He was always very humble and always promoting the idea of peace between the United States and Japan." The community readily accepted him, and he became an honorary citizen of the town.

Fujita's family didn't even know about his actions during the war until he announced his plans to travel to Brookings. Local churches and organizations in Brookings funded that first trip to Oregon, in 1962. Later, Fujita repaid the favor by funding a trip to Japan for three Brookings-Harbor High School students.

Over time, Fujita donated $1,000 to the local library to purchase children's books about Japanese culture. He hoped that building an understanding of the two countries' differences would prevent future wars.

His family's samurai sword is still on display in the community's library. In later visits to the town, Fujita planted trees in the spot where he had dropped the bombs. He died from lung cancer in 1997, knowing that he had been not only forgiven, but also embraced by the small town he had once harmed.

Are You Forgiving?

A friend has just apologized to you for doing something that wasn't nice. Did you accept that apology? If so, then you are forgiving. Being forgiving means that you can stop feeling anger toward someone and stop blaming that person for having done something wrong to you. Forgiving someone is very difficult, but if you can accept someone's apology, then you have taken the first step toward forgiveness.

Kim Phúc

One of the most haunting images from the **Vietnam War** is a photograph of a young girl running away from a chemical attack on her village. The picture captured a horrific moment, and that little girl is still alive today. Her journey through pain and suffering from the burns she received that day led her to forgive those who caused her wounds.

Kim Phúc was born in 1963 in the village of Trang Bang in South Vietnam. She was nine years old when photographer Nick Ut snapped a series of photos of an attack on her village. Immediately after taking the photo, Ut took Kim and the other injured children to a hospital in nearby Saigon. At first, people thought the burns on Kim's back were so severe that she would

During the Vietnam War, soldiers and civilians distrusted each other.

not survive. A journalist found her in critical condition in the local hospital and demanded that she be moved to an American hospital. Another journalist spent 10 years trying to get her out of Vietnam to a hospital in Germany where she could get the surgery she needed. All three men had a part in saving Kim Phúc's life.

Her village had been hit with a napalm bomb. Napalm was a common weapon used in the Vietnam War. It is a **flammable** liquid that sticks to skin while it burns. It was later determined

Napalm could burn down buildings or jungles hiding enemies.

that the napalm bomb was mistakenly dropped on Kim's village. A South Vietnamese Air Force pilot mistook the fleeing villagers as enemy soldiers. "That moment ... will be one Kim Phúc and I will never forget," said photographer Nick Ut. "It has ultimately changed both our lives." Phúc remembers being in tremendous pain and screaming, "It burns, it burns" as she ran.

Today, Phúc lives outside of Toronto, Canada. In 1992, she and her husband received **asylum** there. She gets painful laser treatments in an attempt to reduce some of the scarring she

Kim Phúc and Nick Ut have remained in contact over the years.

Nick Ut's famous photograph of Phúc and her experiences in the Vietnam War convinced many people that the war was wrong.

still has. As a Goodwill Ambassador for the United Nations Educational, Scientific and Cultural Organization (UNESCO), Phúc speaks to groups about how forgiveness has helped her to heal over the years. She explains, "Forgiveness made me free from hatred. I still have many scars on my body and severe pain most days, but my heart is cleansed." In 1997, Phúc established a foundation to provide medical and **psychological** care to children who are victims of war.

In 2012, Phúc attended a gathering of the people who helped to save her life. She said, "It is a miracle. Today I have the opportunity to gather all my heroes who shared my road, to remember what happened that day. They have come from all over the world to celebrate life." Despite years of tremendous pain, Kim Phúc remains very thankful to those who assisted her and forgiving of those who caused her so much suffering. Phúc believes that if everyone could learn to forgive, then war would not exist.

Forgiveness in the Workplace

Being able to forgive is a useful skill in the workplace. Has anyone ever been mean to you because they were having a bad day? Everyone makes mistakes and does mean things they didn't mean to. It's nice to be on good terms with your boss and coworkers because you'll spend a lot of time with them. Forgiveness in the workplace helps you move on from unpleasant moments so that you and your peers can be happy and do your best every day.

Ray Minniecon and the "Stolen Children"

From about 1905 until 1969, thousands of Aboriginal children in Australia were taken from their families and sent to **missions**. This plan, created by the Australian government, was a poor attempt to protect the native people of Australia from dying out. Forced to live among whites until they were 18 years old, most of the children were never reunited with their families. What the plan did instead was cruelly break up families and try and mold the children to be different. The Australian government has only recently apologized to the generations of families it tore apart. Understandably, the Aboriginal people find it difficult to forgive the government for its actions.

The stolen children were not allowed to reunite with their families until after they were 18 years old.

Aboriginal Australians are the **indigenous** people of Australia who lived there before the arrival of Europeans. Much like they did to the Native Americans of North America, white European settlers treated the Aboriginals as an inferior race that needed to be controlled. They sent full-blooded Aboriginal people to **reserves**. Mix-blooded children, referred to as "half-castes," were taken from their parents and sent to church missions. The children spent years there, with the goal of being **assimilated** into white Australian society. White couples adopted these "stolen children." Some young girls were married off to white men.

As of 2017, 3% of Australians are Aboriginal.

Other children were trained to be farm laborers or house servants, and were sent off to work until they were 18 years old.

Ray Minniecon saw many of these forced separations and has devoted his life to the stolen children of Australia. He was one of the lucky Aboriginal children. He was never taken from his family. Minniecon's parents always told him to run if he saw a police car. He remembers hearing "women screaming from one end of the community to the other for their children to run into the bush and hide."

If the goal of the government's program was to improve the

lives of these children, it was far from a success. One study compared these children to Aboriginal children who had grown up in their native community. The study found that the stolen children were less likely to have gone to college, three times as likely to have been arrested, and twice as likely to have used illegal drugs.

In 1997, there was a government report about the effects of taking and trying to assimilate the stolen children. It suggested paying to record the children's individual stories and to make **reparations**. It also recommended that the Australian Parliament apologize and admit responsibility for the government's part in the matter. A national Sorry Day was created. An annual event, its purpose is "to remember and commemorate the mistreatment of the country's indigenous population." But it wasn't practiced until 2008 when Kevin Rudd became prime minister. His first official act was to apologize to the Aboriginal people on behalf of all Australians.

Ray Minniecon accepted the apology because if he "didn't forgive, then the past would always be present." But he still struggles with forgiveness when he remembers what was done to his people. He knows he has to practice forgiveness every day to relieve his bitterness so that he can help others do the same.

CHAPTER 6

Hutus and Tutsis

What if your neighbor wronged you? Could you forgive them? In 1994, two **ethnic** groups in the East African nation of Rwanda had a conflict. The majority group, called the Hutus, harmed the minority group, the Tutsis. Killing a cultural group is called a **genocide**. The conflict lasted 100 days, and many people were hurt and killed. Twenty years later, the families of the people who were harmed met with the people responsible. They wanted to encourage **reconciliation** between the two groups.

Paul Kagame helped end the genocide and became Rwanda's president in 2000.

Maria, a Tutsi, struggled to forgive Juvenal, a Hutu, after he wronged her.

Prior to World War I, Rwanda was a colony of Germany. The treaty that ended the war made Rwanda a **protectorate** of Belgium. Under the rule of both European countries, a class system had been created that gave the Tutsis more power than the Hutus. Clashes between the two groups and clashes against the Belgian government occurred over the years. As a result, there were changes in leadership that led to a civil war erupting in 1990. The killing of Rwanda's Hutu dictator at the end of the war started the genocide. The genocide only ended when a Tutsi rebel group took control of the government and a Tutsi leader took power.

Today, Rwanda has two holidays to recognize and mourn the genocide. And the Association Modeste et Innocent (AMI) is attempting to **reconcile** the two groups. AMI counsels small groups of Tutsis and Hutus for several months, with the goal of having the Hutu **perpetrator** formally request forgiveness. If the surviving Tutsi grants forgiveness, then the Hutu and his family and friends will bring a basket of food and drink to the survivor's family. Photos have been taken of the reconciled individuals, and photographer Pieter Hugo remarked, "There are clearly different degrees of forgiveness." Some Tutsis have found it harder to forgive than others.

But this act of forgiveness is an important step in moving on with their lives. In some cases, Hutus and Tutsis are still neighbors with nowhere else to go. One Tutsi man explained forgiving a man who witnessed the death of his brother and did not try to stop it. "When it comes to forgiveness willingly granted, one is satisfied once and for all," he said. "When someone is full of anger, he can lose his mind. But when I granted forgiveness,

Freda, a Tutsi woman, and Jean Baptiste, a Hutu man, are now friends who help one another on their farms.

I felt my mind at rest." Being forgiven is also good for the perpetrator. "When she granted me pardon, all the things in my heart that had made her look at me like a wicked man faded away," said a Hutu of the woman who forgave him.

The Hutus and Tutsis continue to struggle with their past. But each act of forgiveness helps remind them that they are all Rwandan citizens trying hard to achieve peace.

What Have You Learned About Forgiveness?

Have you ever forgiven someone? Forgiveness is not easy. We all struggle with it. Developing genuine compassion for those who have done us wrong in the past is extremely difficult. But it allows us to move forward instead of letting bitterness and anger ruin our lives. For the person who is asking to be forgiven, the removal of blame is a gift. Without forgiveness, friendships would never be reconciled, fights would go on forever, and war would never end. Practice forgiveness in your daily life and ask others to do the same. The world will be a better place for it.

Think About It

How Can You Become More Forgiving?

The first step to forgiving someone is understanding why they did what they did. You need to listen to that person and understand their side of the story. You also need to tell them how they hurt you. Communication helps lead to forgiveness. Then you can both move on and be happy.

For More Information

Further Reading

Freedman, Russell. *Vietnam: A History of the War.* New York: Holiday House, 2016.

Lowery, Zoe, and Frank Spalding. *The Rwandan Genocide.* New York: Rosen Young Adult, 2016.

Pilkington, Doris. *Follow the Rabbit-Proof Fence.* Brisbane, Australia: University of Queensland Press, 2013.

Websites

Corrie ten Boom House
https://www.corrietenboom.com
This is the official website of the Corrie ten Boom House Museum in the Netherlands.

National Museum of the Pacific War
www.pacificwarmuseum.org
Visit the website of a museum dedicated to sharing the history of the war in the Pacific during World War II.

Splash ABC—Aboriginal and Torres Strait Islander Histories and Cultures
http://splash.abc.net.au/home#!/topic/494038/aboriginal-and-torres-strait-islander-histories-and-cultures
Read about the history and culture of the Aboriginal people of Australia.

GLOSSARY

assimilated (uh-SIM-uh-layt-ed) having been forced to become part of a different society

asylum (uh-SYE-luhm) protection given to someone who has left a dangerous place

captors (KAP-terz) people who captured someone

concentration camp (kahn-suhn-TRAY-shuhn KAMP) a type of prison where large numbers of people are kept during a war and are forced to live in very bad conditions

ethnic (ETH-nik) having to do with a group of people sharing the same national origins, language, or culture

flammable (FLAM-uh-buhl) quick to catch fire and burn

genocide (JEN-uh-side) the deliberate killing of people who belong to a particular racial, political, or cultural group

Holocaust (HAH-luh-kawst) the killing of millions of European Jews and others by the Nazis during World War II

indigenous (in-DIJ-ih-nuhs) originating in a particular region

Jewish (JOO-ish) relating to Judaism, a religion that believes in God

missions (MISH-uhnz) buildings run by people whose intent is to help others or change them in a certain way

perpetrator (PUR-pih-tray-tur) someone who has done something illegal or wrong

protectorate (pruh-TEKT-ur-it) a less powerful country that is controlled and protected by a more powerful one

psychological (sye-kuh-LAH-jih-kuhl) of or relating to the mind

rationing (RASH-uhn-ing) giving out in limited amounts, especially food

reconcile (REK-uhn-sile) to make up or be friendly again after a disagreement

reconciliation (rek-uhn-sil-ee-AY-shuhn) the act of becoming friendly again after an argument or disagreement

reparations (rep-uh-RAY-shuhnz) money that a country or group pays because of the damage, injury, suffering, or deaths it has caused

reserves (ri-ZURVZ) areas of land that a specific group of people are forced to live on

samurai (SAM-uh-rye) a Japanese warrior who lived in medieval times

Vietnam War (vee-et-NAHM WOR) a conflict, starting in 1955 and ending in 1975, between South Vietnam and North Vietnam (and their allies)

INDEX

Aboriginal people, 20–23
apology, 4, 13, 23
Australia, 20–23

blame, 4, 13, 29
bombs, 10–13, 15–16
Brookings, OR, 10–13

communication, 30
compassion, 29
concentration camps, 8–9

forgiveness
    how to practice it, 30
    what it does, 29
    what it is, 4–5, 13
    in the workplace, 19
Fujita, Nobuo, 10–13

genocide, 6–7, 24–29

Hutus, 24–29

Japan, 10–13
Jewish people, 6–9

Kagame, Paul, 25

listening, 30

Minniecon, Ray, 20–23

napalm, 15–16
Nazis, 6–9
Netherlands, 6–9

Phúc, Kim, 14–19

Rwanda, 24–29

Sorry Day, 23
"stolen children," 20–23

ten Boom, Corrie, 6–9
Tutsis, 24–29

Ut, Nick, 14, 16, 17

Vietnam War, 14–19

World War II, 6–9, 10–13